THE FRIED PIPER
of HAMSTRING

Written by Laurence Anholt
Illustrated by Arthur Robins

ORCHARD BOOKS
338 Euston Road,
London NW1 3BH
Orchard Books Australia
Hachette Children's Books
Level 17/207 Kent Street, Sydney, NSW 2000
First published in Great Britain in 1998. This edition published in 2002
Text © Laurence Anholt 1998. Illustrations © Arthur Robins 1998.
The rights of Laurence Anholt to be identified as the author
and Arthur Robins as the illustrator of this work
have been asserted by them in accordance with the
Copyright, Designs and Patents Act, 1988.
A CIP catalogue record for this book is available from the British Library.
ISBN 978 1 84121 398 9

☆ The Fried Piper ☆ Shampoozel ☆ Daft Jack ☆ The Emperor ☆
☆ Little Red Riding Wolf ☆ Rumply Crumply Stinky Pin ☆

☆ Ghostyshocks ☆ Snow White ☆ Cinderboy ☆ Eco-Wolf ☆
☆ The Greedy Farmer ☆ Billy Beast ☆

The grown ups in Hamstring Town were
the bossiest people in the ENTIRE
UNIVERSE.

They would never leave
their kids alone…

It never ever stopped.

The grown ups had rules for everything.
Every child had to know them by heart:

No toys, no TV, no treats.
No singing, no swinging, no sweets.

The grown ups were especially strict about the fried food.

"All those greasy chips and hamburgers will give you spots and make you lazy," they would tell their little ones.

So the poor children of Hamstring were allowed only organic fruit and vegetables, three times a day, and NO snacks between meals.

Everything in Hamstring Town was spick and span. Little girls had shiny hair in pretty bows. Boys wore short trousers until their thirty-fifth birthday, even if their legs were hairy. In the evening, families had spelling tests together.

It was boring.
It was gloomy.
It was DULL!

But, of all the bossy grown ups in Hamstring Town, no one was stricter than the Mayor.

The Mayor of Hamstring spent all his time inventing new rules to make things even tidier. He didn't like children and he especially hated animals.

"Animals are so messy," he would snarl.
"Let's have a new law. From now on, all
cows must be toilet trained.

"And BIRDS..." he shouted "...birds are
dirty little creatures. From today all birds
must wear nappies."

The boys and girls of Hamstring would have given anything for their own little puppy or a baby hamster or even a stick insect, but pets were strictly forbidden in Hamstring Town.

As the days passed, things got worse and worse.

On Monday the Mayor banned music, moustaches and morris men.

On Tuesday he banned chewing gum, chocolate and chattering.

On Wednesday he banned watches, weeds and whispering.

On Thursday he banned theatres, thunderstorms and thinking.

On Friday he banned freckles, frogs and fireworks.

On Saturday he banned scratching,
scarecrows and smiling.

On Sunday – well, on Sunday some of the
children sneaked off to meet secretly.

"This has gone too far," whispered one of the big children. "Soon there will be nothing left to ban. We must do something NOW. We must stop that mad Mayor."

"We need some help," said a little girl at the back.

"Yes," said a boy. "We need a person who isn't afraid of grown ups."

So the children typed out a secret message. It said:

> **S.O.S.**
> **Hamstring kids urgently require**
> **A FEARLESS HERO**
> **to save the town**
> **from a power-mad mayor**
> **and too many RULES!**
> **HELP! Come quick.**

The children sent the message out to every newspaper in the land.

They sent it by e-mail. They faxed it.
They sent it out on the Internet. **'Replies to:
www.rulebuster@hamstring.com'**

Then they went home for tea.

At first light, as the children wandered wearily to school, they spotted a strange figure high on a mountain top above the town.

The children could tell straight away that
the stranger was not from their town
because he was dressed in the most
extraordinary way.

Instead of grey shorts, he wore red and yellow jeans and a bomber jacket to match. His hair was tied in a ponytail; a gleaming gold saxophone hung round his neck. Most outrageous of all, the boy was sitting on a dazzling mountain bike.

To the children's amazement, the stranger leapt on to the saddle and hurtled down the hillside to where they were standing.

In a great cloud of dust, the bike spun to a halt.

It was only then that the children realised the stranger was holding something in his gloved hands…

Something terrible… Something so wicked, it was banned throughout all Hamstring…

…A Mega-Burger with French Fries, all
sprinkled with salt and dripping with
tomato ketchup!

A gasp ran through the crowd.

The children stared wide-eyed as the boy
began to speak in strange musical words:
"I was out on my bike, just takin' a cruise,
I nearly freaked out when I heard the news.

"Said, 'I'll hit the road and burn on down,
To help those dudes in Hamstring Town.'

"Yeah, I'm the Fried Piper and I am hip,
Any of you cool cats care for...A CHIP?"

The children of Hamstring stood frozen.
They couldn't believe their eyes.

Then, very slowly, a tiny boy stepped forward. He looked around, and, quick as a flash, he grabbed a chip from the Fried Piper's outstretched hand and stuffed it into his mouth.

It was the first chip he had ever eaten. And it was DELICIOUS!

In a second, everyone had gathered round, stuffing chips into their mouths, laughing and chattering and admiring the beautiful bike.

"But...but are you really allowed a bike?" someone asked. "What about The Rules?"

The Fried Piper only laughed and tossed
back his golden hair.

*"You know, rules ain't cool. I do what I like,
I dig fried food and I LOVE my bike.*

*"If you follow me, then pretty soon,
You'll hear me blowin' a RADICAL tune!"*

The children knew they should be at school, but somehow, they couldn't help it. They *had* to follow that wonderful smell of fried chips and tomato sauce. The Fried Piper led them slowly down the road towards the centre of Hamstring Town.

At that moment, the wicked Mayor was searching for children who were late for school. Suddenly he heard an unusual noise. It sounded like scurrying feet. It sounded like chattering. It sounded like laughing. It sounded like…CHILDREN!

The Mayor spun around.

"ARE YOU MAD?" he shouted. "This is SCHOOL TIME. Have you forgotten Rule 48B, Subsection 19? It clearly says that any child absent from school for any reason shall…"

The Mayor stopped. He stared. His jaw hung open. The Fried Piper stepped out of the crowd. He pushed his bike into the town square, where the sun cast long shadows…

"HEY! You Mayor. You big fat dude,
We don't dig your rules, we don't dig your food.

"You got too much belly and not enough hair,
You're what I call a real NIGHT MAYOR!"

The children began to laugh. They just couldn't stop.

The Mayor struggled for something to say.
He turned red. The children laughed more.

At last the Mayor blurted out, "THIS…
THIS IS AN OUTRAGE! Where are your
shorts, young man? There are rules…
RULES…RULES!!"

Slowly,
the Fried Piper
stepped forward.
He leaned his bike
carefully against a railing. His long fingers
drummed on his saxophone. His dark eyes
fixed on the Mayor. A strange silence fell
over the town.

In a firm, low voice the stranger
whispered,
  *"Chill out, Mayor. That's enough of your threats,
   Us kids need fun and we need…PETS!"*

At the sound of the word 'pets', the Mayor
gasped.

The Piper put his gleaming gold
instrument to his lips and began to play –
a weird haunting tune which rose up above
the houses and all across the mountains
around Hamstring Town.

Everyone stood in silence, until they heard a faint, distant squeaking. To the Mayor's horror, a tiny baby rat came scampering along the main street, sniffing the air and twitching its little whiskers.

The rat was followed by
a guinea pig. The guinea
pig by a hamster.
Behind the hamster
bounced two long-
eared rabbits. The
rabbits were followed
by kittens. The kittens
by puppies.

And still the Piper played on.

The children of Hamstring scooped up the little animals and started to stroke and kiss them.

The Mayor began to shake.
"The Rules," he croaked. "The Rules…"
But the Fried Piper didn't miss a note.

More and more pets came hopping and bounding into the main square of Hamstring. Big and small. Tortoises, budgies, ponies. Parrots, dogs, cats. Squeaking, yapping, barking. Whistling, grunting, yelping.

The children were delighted. They ran to meet the new animals who jumped up and licked their happy faces. Behind the noise, the strange tune continued.

Donkeys, goats, monkeys. Lizards, lambs, frogs. Rolling, running, racing. Scurrying, scampering, chasing.

A large dog licked the Mayor's ear. A monkey climbed onto his hat. The Mayor put his hands to his face and began to weep. "The Rules," he sobbed. "Oh, the Rules…"

The bossy grown ups of Hamstring had been watching their children in dismay. Now they turned and ran. Down the street and out of the town. Over the mountains and far far away.

Only one person could not keep up. The Mayor ran as fast as his fat little legs would carry him, but as he reached the edge of the mountains, a huge kangaroo bounded after him.

She scooped him up and shoved him into her pouch.

As they bounded back to town, the Mayor squealed, "NO KANGAROOS! NO HOPPING! NO BOUNCING!"

That evening, there was great feasting in Hamstring. The children lit a fire in the town square and the Mayor was made to cook the most enormous fry-up of all time: fried eggs, fried bread, fried bananas and - most of all - hundreds and thousands of chips, dripping in tomato sauce.

Late into the night, the children and
their pets danced to the wild tunes of the
Fried Piper.

The party lasted four long days. When it was over, the grown ups crept quietly home from their hiding places in the mountains.

The Mayor was still busy cleaning the
frying pan.

So the Fried Piper made one or two rules
of his own.

Gather round dudes, here's my number one rule :
Think for yourself and you'll always be cool.

Like what you do and do what you like.
Hey! Anyone seen my mountain bike?

And the Fried Piper rode away into the sunset.

To this very day there are no rules in
Hamstring town. The people do exactly
what they please. They are the coolest cats
for miles around.

And the hippest, smoothest, most radical dude of them all is…

...that crazy old Mayor himself.

THE VALE OF SAD BANANA

That summer in Rustum Magna, the hot, dry days had lasted far longer than usual, and the superstitious villagers began seeking explanations. Some admitted to feelings of unease one particularly hot night. Dr Ritchie knew that their fears were by no means groundless. His instruments recorded a jolt in the earth's rotation that night — the same night that the Ministry of Defence lost contact with its most dangerous space weapon. But most of all, Dr Ritchie feared the uncanny intelligence of his young helper, Bobby Miller . . .